UNITED STATES

D1420597

This book provides a clear informative introduction to the exciting world of space. It describes the stars, planets and other bodies that make up the Universe and looks at space exploration and travel.

Acknowledgments:
The publishers would like to thank Wendy Body for acting as reading level consultant and Douglas Arnold for advising on scientific content.

Photographic credits:
Page 13, Akira Fujii; pages 8 (2), 12, H. J. P. Arnold/Space Frontiers Limited; page 37, ESA/Space Frontiers Limited; page 22, Kenneth Fountayne; pages 19 (2), 20, 28, 29, 35 bottom, 39, 42 right, 43 right, NASA/Space Frontiers Limited; cover, Spacecharts; pages 35 top, 42 left, 43 left, TASS/Space Frontiers Limited.

British Library Cataloguing in Publication Data

Daly, Bridget
    Space.
    1. Outer space
    I. Title   II. Kerrod, Robin   III. Watson, Brian
    523
    ISBN 0-7214-1106-1

First edition

Published by Ladybird Books Ltd Loughborough Leicestershire UK
Ladybird Books Inc Auburn Maine 04210 USA

© LADYBIRD BOOKS LTD MCMLXXXIX

Printed in England

Space

written by BRIDGET DALY
and ROBIN KERROD
illustrated by BRIAN WATSON

Ladybird Books

Into space

Climb into your seat in the space shuttle and prepare for lift-off! The rocket engines fire and the shuttle thunders into the sky. In seconds you see the clouds flash by. The air outside gets thinner as the rocket climbs. Suddenly the air has been left behind and you are in space.

Looking at Earth from space you can see a fuzzy blue band round its edge. This is Earth's layer of air or **atmosphere**. This layer is about 100 km high.

The sky at night contains about 3,000 stars that you can see without having to use binoculars or a telescope.

Space and our galaxy

Earth and eight other planets are part of a **solar system**. Every solar system has a star at its centre. Our star is the Sun.

Our solar system is just a tiny part of a huge cloud of stars called a **galaxy**.

Our galaxy, the Milky Way, contains about 100,000 million stars and is about 100,000 **light years** across.

The **Universe** is made up of millions of galaxies.

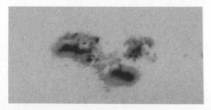

Cooler parts on the Sun's surface form darker patches or **sunspots**.

Jets of gas often stream away from the surface of the Sun. Sometimes we see them as **flares** or ribbons of gas called **prominences**.

Our star, the Sun

Stars are huge balls of hot glowing gases. They come in many colours, including red, yellow, blue and white. Our Sun is a medium-sized yellow star. It looks large to us because it is much closer than any other star in our galaxy. The Sun gives Earth light and heat. Without it we could not survive.

The temperature at the Sun's surface is 6,000 °C. In the centre it is even hotter — 15 million °C. Water boils at 100 °C.

The solar system

Everything in space is moving. The Earth spins round on its **axis** like a top. It completes one spin every 24 hours. At the same time it travels round the Sun in a huge oval path called an **orbit**. Each orbit takes a year. Mercury orbits the Sun in only 88 days, but Pluto takes almost 248 years.

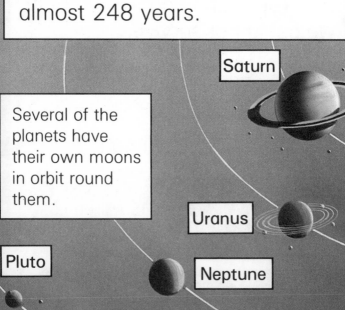

Several of the planets have their own moons in orbit round them.

Saturn

Uranus

Pluto

Neptune

The Sun is almost 1.4 million km across. You could fit more than a million Earths inside it. Because the Sun is so big, it pulls all objects within about 6,000 million km and beyond into orbit round it.

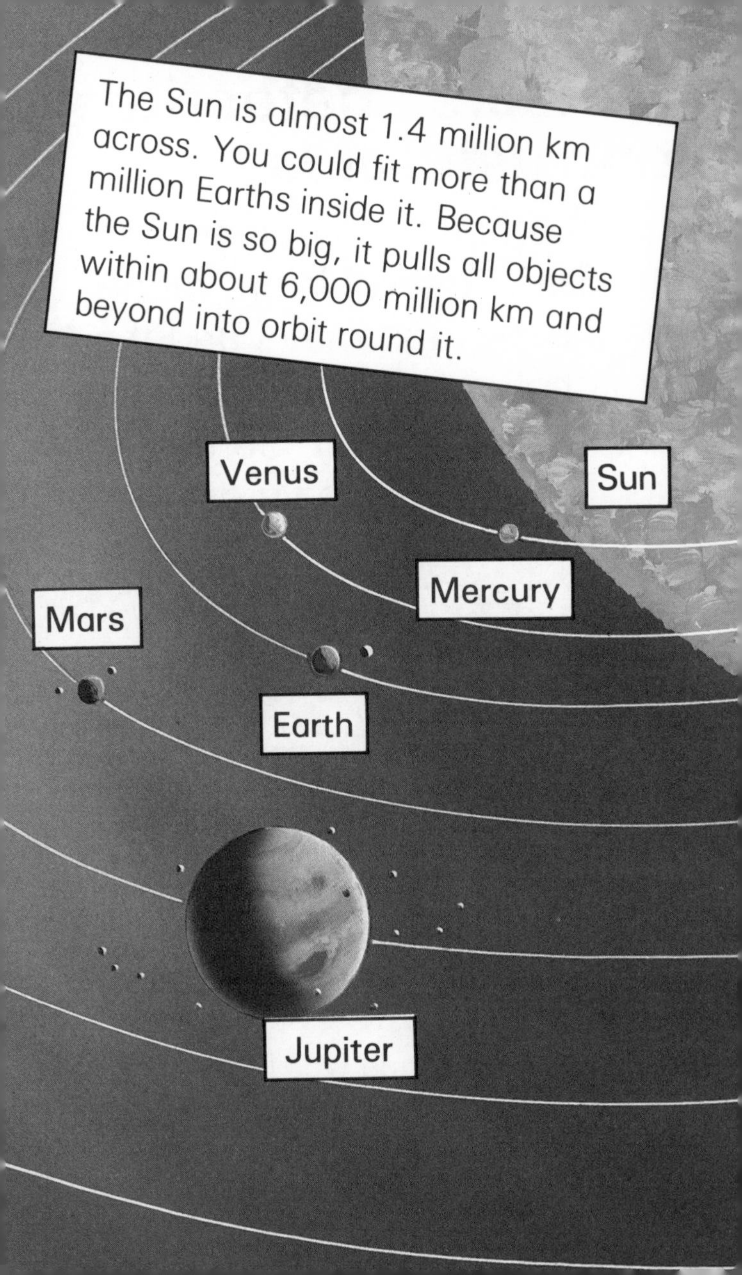

Venus

Sun

Mercury

Mars

Earth

Jupiter

Meteors, meteorites and asteroids

Many other small objects circle the Sun. **Asteroids** are made from rocks and metal and they orbit between Mars and Jupiter in the asteroid belt. Sometimes, space dust falls towards Earth.

This crater in Arizona was formed 50,000 years ago when a meteorite 80 m wide fell to Earth.

Some pieces, called **meteors**, burn up in the atmosphere. Other pieces, called **meteorites**, pass through the atmosphere and hit the Earth's surface.

Meteors burn up in the atmosphere and are often called shooting stars. At certain times, showers of meteors can be seen in the sky.

Asteroids can be smaller than a football or as large as Britain. The largest one is called Ceres.

The inner planets

Earth, Mercury, Venus and Mars are the four inner planets, those closest to the Sun. Except for Pluto, they are the smallest in the solar system. Mercury, Venus and Mars are made mainly of rock, with dry surfaces. Scientists have found life on only one planet – Earth.

The nearest planet to the Sun is Mercury. It has no air or water. The side facing the Sun is hot enough to melt lead. The other side is freezing cold.

Venus is covered in clouds of poisonous gases, which trap the sunlight. This makes Venus unbearably hot.

Nearly three quarters of the Earth's surface is covered in water.

Mars is known as the red planet because it has large deserts of red dust.

The giant planet Jupiter is eleven times bigger than Earth. It is mostly made up of gas and the giant red spot is probably a huge storm.

Saturn is circled by many beautiful rings made of rock and ice.

Icy Uranus looks bluish-green because of the kind of gas in its atmosphere. It has eleven faint rings.

The outer planets

On the far side of the asteroid belt are the outer planets – Jupiter, Saturn, Uranus and Neptune. They are made up of layers of gases. Pluto, the planet furthest from the Sun, is very different – it is small with a solid surface.

Neptune is thought to be a world with rock and ice at its centre. Like Uranus, it is surrounded by a bluish-green gas.

Pluto

Earth

Frozen Pluto is less than a quarter the size of Earth. It was not discovered until 1930.

The Moon

Like many planets, Earth has a **satellite**, the Moon, which orbits Earth once every 27 days. The Moon has no air and no water on its surface. In the day it is boiling hot but at night it is freezing.

Orbit of the Moon round Earth

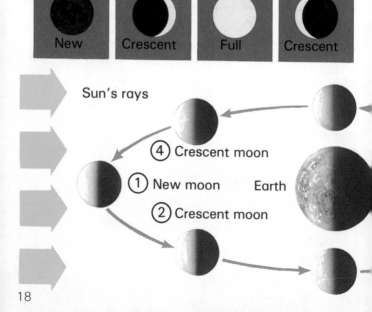

1 New	2 Crescent	3 Full	4 Crescent

Sun's rays

④ Crescent moon

① New moon   Earth

② Crescent moon

Much of the Moon's surface is a greyish dust, pitted with craters made by meteorites falling from space.

The dark patches on the Moon's "face" are huge plains. The bright patches are mountains.

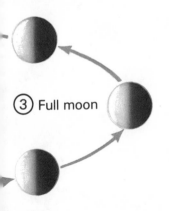

③ Full moon

When the Moon lies between the Sun and Earth, we cannot see it. As it orbits Earth we can see more of the Moon as more of its surface is lit up by the Sun.

Destination – the Moon

On 20th July 1969 the American spacecraft *Apollo 11* landed on the Moon. A few hours later Neil Armstrong, one of two **astronauts**, stepped out onto its surface. Since then eleven other Americans have walked, worked and slept on the Moon, 384,000 km away in space.

It took almost ten years of planning to put people on the Moon. First, scientists had to send robot spacecraft to see where a spacecraft could land safely.

The first astronauts landed in a **lunar module**.

Because there is no wind or rain on the Moon, a human footprint will remain for a very long time.

One small step
The first words Armstrong spoke when he stepped onto the Moon were: ''That's one small step for a man, one giant leap for mankind.''

Rocket power

Everything on Earth is held down by a force called **gravity**. To overcome this force, rockets

Firework rockets
Firework rockets use gunpowder for fuel. The hot gases that form as the gunpowder burns push the rocket upwards.

The Russian rocket *Energia* is the most powerful in the world. It can carry up to 100 tonnes – as much as fifteen full grown elephants.

need a lot of power. To leave Earth's surface and enter orbit rockets must reach a speed of at least 28,000 km an hour – ten times the speed of a bullet!

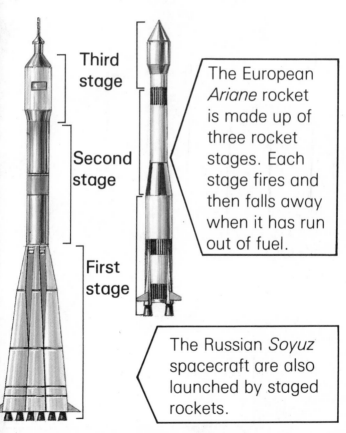

Third stage

Second stage

First stage

The European *Ariane* rocket is made up of three rocket stages. Each stage fires and then falls away when it has run out of fuel.

The Russian *Soyuz* spacecraft are also launched by staged rockets.

The fuel tank carries liquid oxygen and hydrogen. These fuels are burnt by the orbiter's main engines.

The solid rocket boosters burn solid fuel. They fire for the first two minutes only, and lift the shuttle away from Earth.

The space shuttle

The space shuttle first went into orbit in April 1981. It flew again in November 1981 and became the first spacecraft to make two journeys into space.

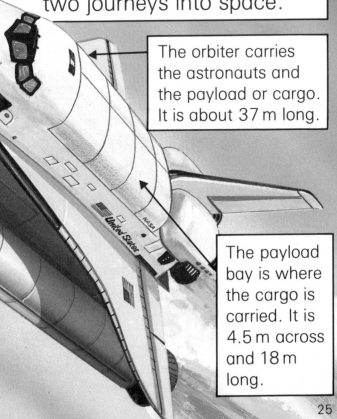

The orbiter carries the astronauts and the payload or cargo. It is about 37 m long.

The payload bay is where the cargo is carried. It is 4.5 m across and 18 m long.

The space shuttle

The American space shuttle was the first spacecraft that could be re-used.

It is part rocket, part spacecraft and part aircraft.

It takes off like a rocket, acts like a spacecraft in space and lands on a runway like an aircraft.

Boosters away!

2 After lift-off the boosters separate and fall to Earth. The main engines carry on firing.

Lift-off

1 The shuttle's main engines and boosters fire together.

3 Then the fuel tank separates and burns up as it falls to Earth. The shuttle goes on into orbit.

4 The orbiter carries people and equipment. Here, it launches a satellite with its robot arm.

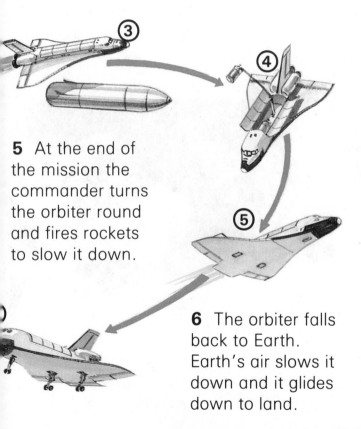

5 At the end of the mission the commander turns the orbiter round and fires rockets to slow it down.

6 The orbiter falls back to Earth. Earth's air slows it down and it glides down to land.

Training an astronaut

Astronauts or cosmonauts have to train for many months before they are ready to go into space. They also need to know what to do in an emergency and how all the equipment on board works.

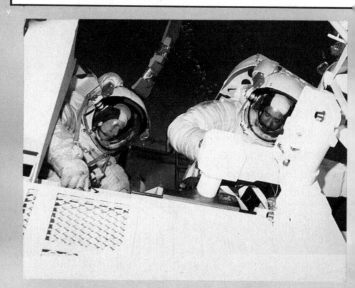

Astronauts train in dummy spacecraft, which are like real ones.

In space everything is weightless and floats around. This can be fun but after a while it can weaken the astronauts' bones and muscles. Astronauts need to do special exercises.

Astronauts fly fast jets to practise the skills they will need to fly spacecraft.

Living in space

Life in space is quite difficult because there is no gravity. You cannot walk properly because your feet don't stay on the floor. If you eat a dry biscuit it breaks into crumbs which float away. If you try to drink orange juice from a glass, it either stays in the glass or floats away in droplets!

Shuttle astronauts eat their food on a tray with a knife and fork, like on an aircraft.

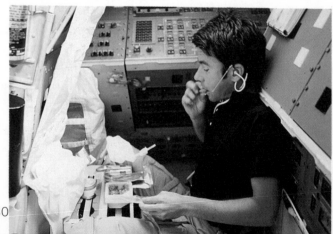

Astronauts sleep zipped up in a sleeping bag.

An astronaut checks the instruments in his spacecraft.

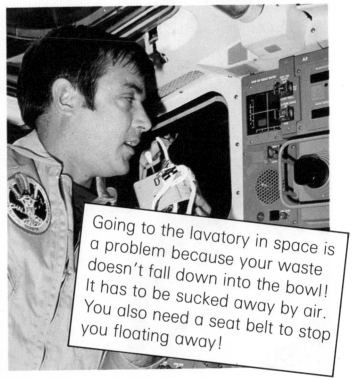

Going to the lavatory in space is a problem because your waste doesn't fall down into the bowl! It has to be sucked away by air. You also need a seat belt to stop you floating away!

Space walking

Sometimes astronauts have to go outside their spacecraft to do experiments or repairs. This is called space walking. They have to wear a special suit or they would die. The suit must be very strong to protect them. There is no air in space so the suit must carry oxygen for the astronaut to breathe.

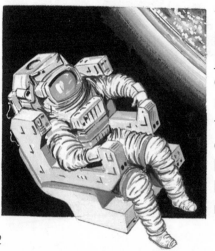

This astronaut is in a sort of jet-propelled chair. He moves by firing little jets of gas out of his backpack, like mini rockets.

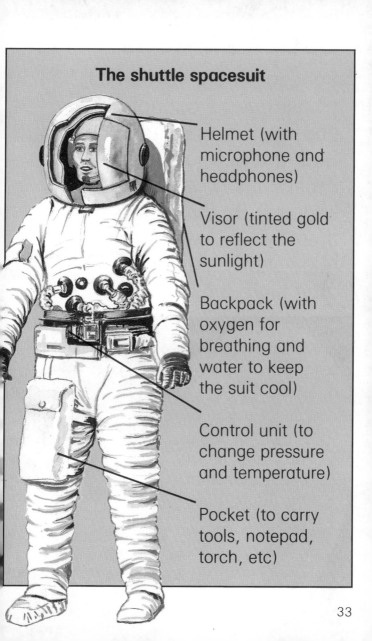

The shuttle spacesuit

Helmet (with microphone and headphones)

Visor (tinted gold to reflect the sunlight)

Backpack (with oxygen for breathing and water to keep the suit cool)

Control unit (to change pressure and temperature)

Pocket (to carry tools, notepad, torch, etc)

Space stations

Spacecraft are very small, so astronauts cannot live and work in them for long. Both the Russians and Americans have built space stations. By the year 2000 there will probably be two huge space stations in orbit high above Earth.

An international space station of the future may look like this.

This Russian space scientist is having his dinner aboard one of the *Salyut* space stations.

The American space station *Skylab* was launched in 1973 and was very large. It fell back to Earth in July 1979.

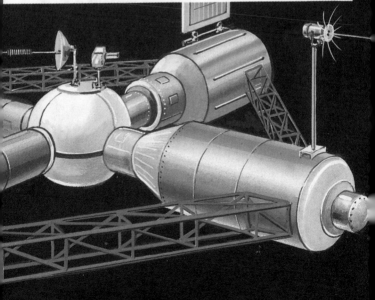

Working satellites

Man-made satellites are spacecraft that circle in space round Earth. They do not carry people, but do all sorts of jobs.

Communication satellites, or comsats, pass telephone and television signals round the world. Signals are beamed up to them and then sent back to receiving stations on Earth.

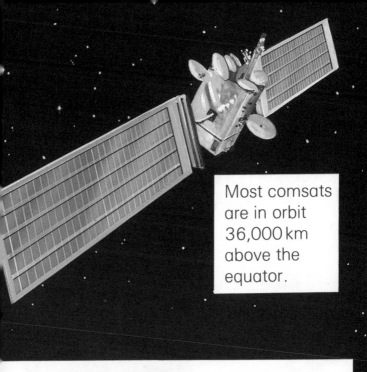

Most comsats are in orbit 36,000 km above the equator.

Computers are often used to improve satellite pictures of Earth showing the weather patterns.

Space probes

Space **probes** are robot explorers sent to study the planets in our solar system. They can go to places that are too dangerous or too far away for humans. They carry out many tasks and sometimes carry cameras to take pictures.

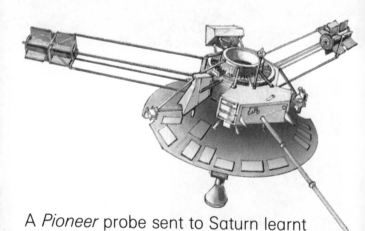

A *Pioneer* probe sent to Saturn learnt that winds can blow at speeds of up to 1,500 km an hour.

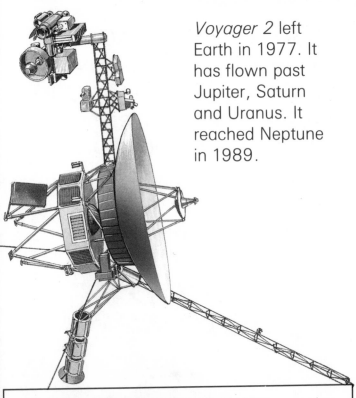

Voyager 2 left Earth in 1977. It has flown past Jupiter, Saturn and Uranus. It reached Neptune in 1989.

Two *Viking* probes landed on Mars. They took pictures of the red dusty surface and reported on the Martian weather.

Is anyone out there?

At this moment four space probes are speeding far out into space. They carry messages for any living being that might one

Some people say that they have seen strange objects (UFOs) flying in the sky. Others say that they have spoken to strange beings in silver suits.

day find them. But are there any other living beings in space? Many scientists think there are. They might live on planets like Earth, orbiting other stars like our Sun.

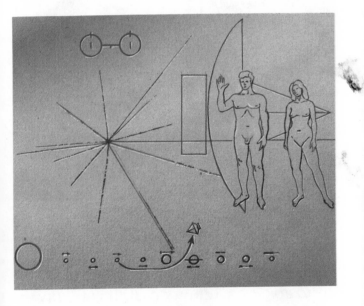

Two *Pioneer* space probes are carrying a picture message like this. It shows what human beings look like and where Earth is situated in space.

Space firsts

The space age began on 4th October 1957 when Russia launched the first satellite,

Yuri Gagarin, a Russian, orbited Earth in 108 minutes in *Vostok 1* on 12th April 1961. The manned part of *Vostok* was only about 2 m across.

John Glenn, an American, made three orbits of Earth on 20th February 1962. His trip in a *Mercury* capsule, *Friendship 7,* lasted nearly five hours.

Sputnik 1, into orbit round Earth. Four years later in 1961 Russia launched the first man into space.

The first woman in space was Valentina Tereshkova. She flew in a Russian spacecraft called *Vostok 6* on 16th June 1963.

In June 1965 Edward White, an American, went outside the *Gemini* spacecraft and spent 21 minutes ''walking'' in space.

Glossary of some words you need to know

asteroid A minor planet made of rock or metal orbiting the Sun.

astronaut A human being who travels in space. Russian astronauts are called cosmonauts.

atmosphere The layer of gases surrounding a planet or star.

axis An imaginary line passing through Earth's centre, round which Earth turns.

flare A storm on the Sun which flings off hot gas into space.

galaxy A group of millions of stars held together by gravity.

gravity A force that pulls objects towards each other.

light year The distance light travels in a year.

lunar module The part of the spacecraft used by the *Apollo* astronauts to land on the Moon.

meteor A speck of space dust that burns up in Earth's atmosphere.

meteorite Small pieces of rock or metal that hit Earth's surface.

orbit A path made in space by one object going round another.

probe A machine sent from Earth to study objects in space.

prominence A sheet of glowing gas seen above the Sun's surface.

satellite A natural or man-made object which orbits a larger object in space.

solar system A star and all the objects that orbit round it.

sunspots Areas of cooler gas on the Sun.

Universe The whole of space and all the objects in it.